DOT THE FIRE DOG

DOT THE FIRE DOG

DOT

THE

FIRE DOG

LISA DESIMINI

SCHOLASTIC INC.

NEW YORK   TORONTO   LONDON   AUCKLAND   SYDNEY
MEXICO CITY   NEW DELHI   HONG KONG   BUENOS AIRES

ISBN 0-439-45229-5

This book was originally published in hardcover by
the Blue Sky Press in 2001.

12 11 10 9 8 7 6 5 4 3 2 1   2 3 4 5 6 7/0

Printed in the U.S.A.   14

First Scholastic paperback printing, September 2002

Designed by Lisa Desimini and Kathleen Westray

For all
junior firefighters,
especially
Robert Martin Staenberg

Dot the fire dog
lives in the firehouse and
sleeps by the firefighters'
big rubber boots.

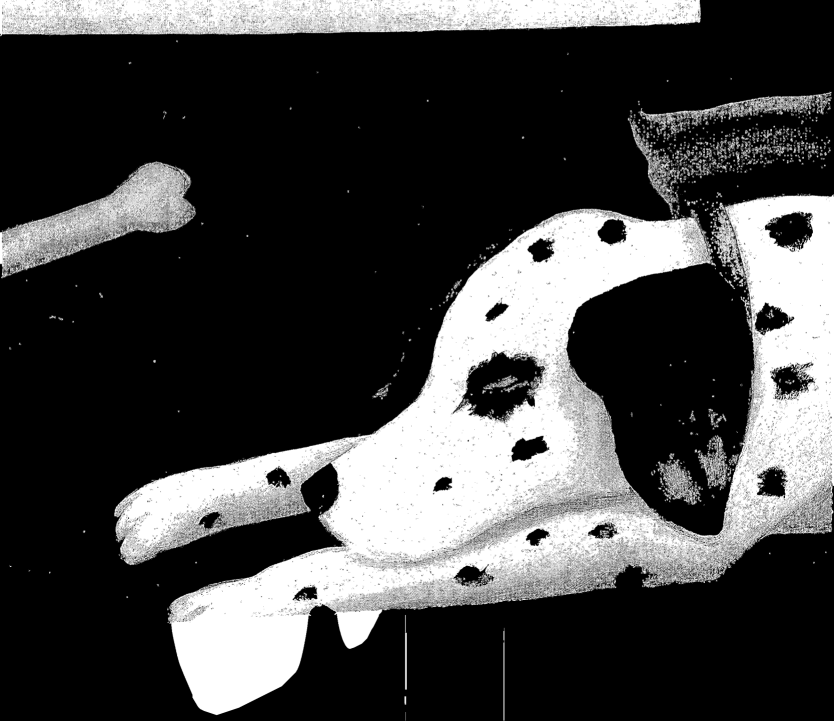

Their black jackets
with yellow stripes hang on hooks
next to their helmets

while the big red
fire truck
waits downstairs.

The firefighters
might be . . .
stirring a pot
of spaghetti,
or reading a book,
or playing catch
with Dot, when . . .

RRRRRRRRRRRRRRING!
Everyone stops.
Now they move fast.
They pull on their
big rubber boots and
put on their pants
and their jackets.
Don't forget
your helmets.
You, too,
Dot.

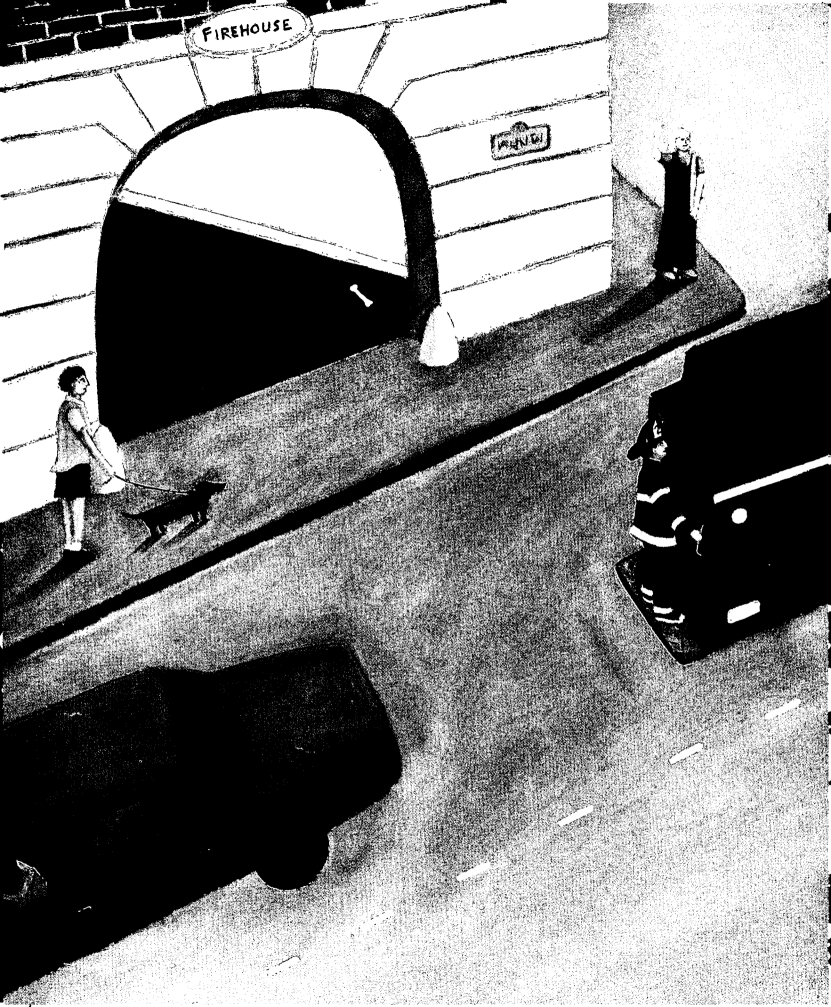

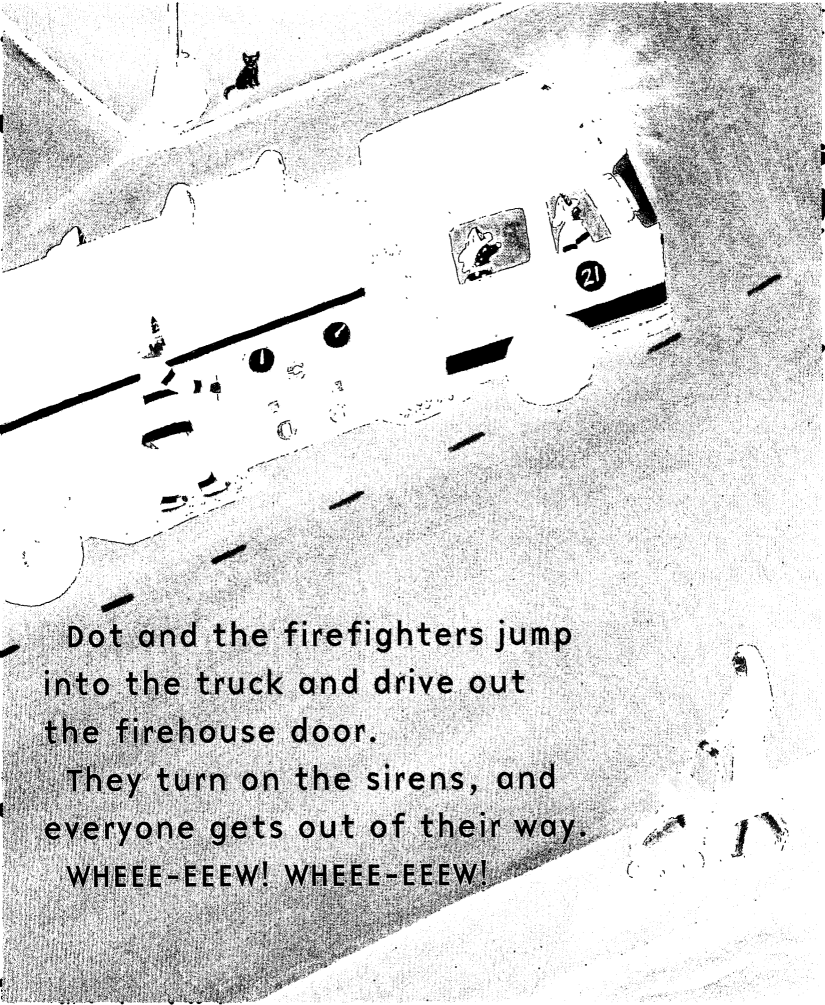

Dot and the firefighters jump
into the truck and drive out
the firehouse door.
They turn on the sirens, and
everyone gets out of their way.
WHEEE-EEEW! WHEEE-EEEW!

The fire truck stops in front
of the burning house.

Dot and a firefighter run inside to wake up an old man who is sick in bed. The firefighter carries him to safety.

Oh, no! Dot hears a kitten.
It must be trapped
inside the house.

Dot goes back. She comes out
carrying the little kitten
in her mouth.

A firefighter climbs the ladder
and breaks a window to let
the smoke out.

Down below, it takes
three firefighters to aim
the water at the windows.

It takes a while but finally the fire is out.

The firefighters load their gear
onto the truck.
The old man is feeling better.
He thanks the firefighters, and
the little kitten licks Dot's nose.

Back at the firehouse, the firefighters step out of their boots and pants and hang up their jackets next to their helmets. Dot's helmet comes off, too.

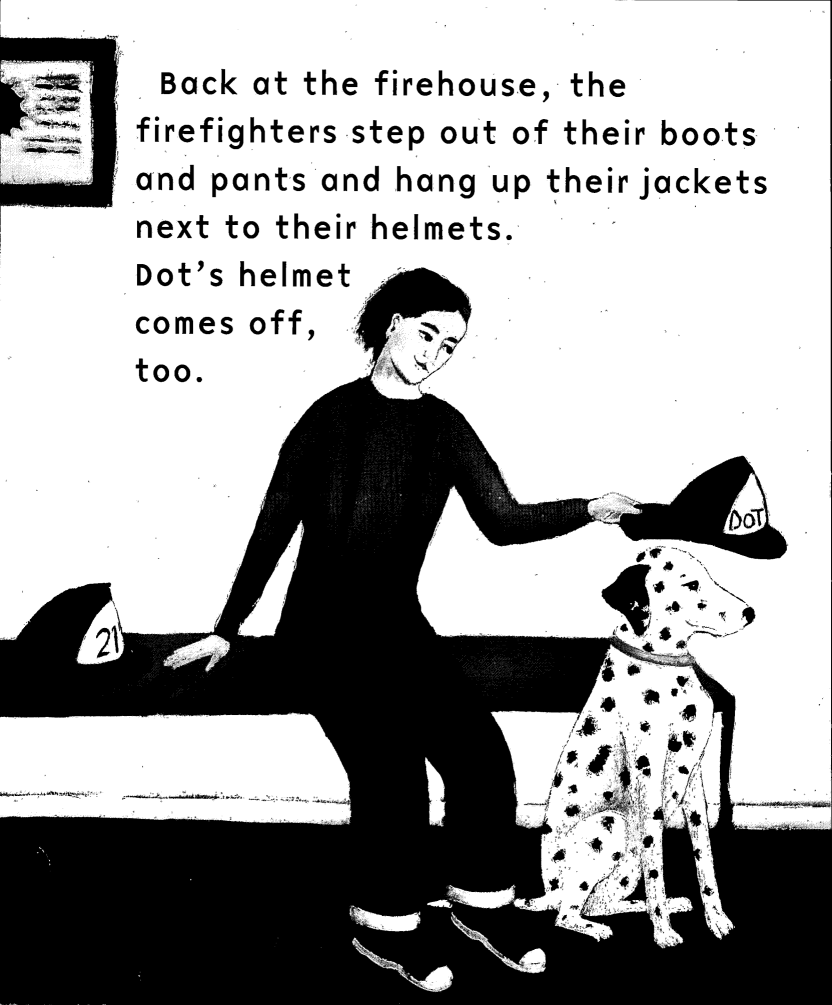

Everything gets checked out
and put away. The truck
gets washed outside,
behind the station.

Now, the
firefighters can
rest after a job well done.
They might . . .
play a game of checkers,
or eat a bowl of soup.
Dot takes a nap next to
the big rubber boots
. . . but she will
be ready when
the alarm bell
rings again.

Dot's Fire Safety Tips

Don't play with matches, lighters, lit candles, stoves, or fire.

Have smoke detectors throughout your house or building, and test them each month.

At the first sign of a fire or the sound of your fire alarm, go outside quickly to safety. If you can't get out, stay low to the ground. Don't hide. Stay where firefighters can find you.

Do not go back into the building—no matter what.

Tell an adult about the fire.

Know your local emergency number—often 911.

Set up an escape plan with your family, and practice it. Plan where your family will meet outside.

If the air is filled with too much smoke, crawl on the floor so you won't breathe in the smoke.

Touch any closed doors (not doorknobs—they can burn you) with the back of your hand. Do not open them if they are hot. Find another way out.

If your clothes catch fire, stop, drop to the ground, and roll. Do not run.